P9-ANZ-317

Dick Whittington

A story from England

RETOLD FOR THIS EDITION BY
CHARLES CAUSLEY

ILLUSTRATED BY ANTONY MAITLAND

PUFFIN BOOKS

Puffin Books,
Penguin Books Ltd,
Harmondsworth, Middlesex, England
Penguin Books,
625 Madison Avenue, New York, New York 10022,
U.S.A.
Penguin Books Australia Ltd,
Ringwood, Victoria, Australia
Penguin Books Canada Ltd,
41 Steelcase Road West, Markham, Ontario, Canada
Penguin Books (N.Z.) Ltd,
182-190 Wairau Road, Auckland 10, New Zealand

Published in Puffin books 1976

Made and printed in Italy by
Garzanti Editore, Milan

An Andreas Landshoff Book

Half a thousand years ago and more, there lived a poor orphan boy of Gloucestershire by the name of Dick Whittington.

Poor he may have been, but he was as pleasant a lad as had ever been known in the village of Pauntley. Dependable as the morning, he cheered friend and neighbour with the warmth of his nature as did the rising sun itself. He was sturdy of limb, dark of hair and eye, and with a gaze as straight as light. And if there was one word in the language which Dick did not seem to know the meaning of, that word was 'laziness'.

But, sadly, it became clear to him that there was not enough work in the village for those able enough to perform it. Every day, his mite of food grew smaller, and a halfpenny was as rare as an English rose in midwinter.

So one morning, long before the cock cleared its metal throat to announce the first of day, Dick set out to walk to London. There, he had been told, every citizen was either a grand lady or gentleman; every house was of pure, white stone that shone like silver; and, best of all, the paving-stones were made of gold.

When he reached the city, the tall sky, what he could

see of it, was the same homely ceiling of blue he had
known all his life in Gloucestershire. But the houses
on either side of the streets, their jutting windows
thrusting ever closer together as they rose towards the
heavens, all but blocked out the sun and the light. The
air he breathed was tainted by the smoke from a

thousand housefires and workshops.
Every building was stained the colour
of soot, and so were many of the
faces of the Londoners as they
hastened about their business. And
what a hurry they were all in, to be
sure!

None had a word for the country
boy, with his friendly greeting.
Rather, they stared at him when
he spoke as though he had mislaid
his wits, or would have done them
a mischief; and they rushed even
faster upon their various ways.

Now if all the people of London
had been noble lords and ladies, as

Dick had been led to expect, he might have understood this better. For why, he would have thought, should rich and important people trouble to pause in their affairs and reply to a humble, poor boy such as he? But if all the people of London were great ladies and lords, they certainly didn't look it. Most of them were dressed as poorly as Dick himself and, not a few, even worse.

To turn his mind from hunger, Dick thought it time to discover some pavements made of gold, in the hope that a fragment of one might buy him a loaf, or even a pie, for his supper. So he set off cheerfully in search, sure that good fortune would attend him before long.

Alas, though many a street did he wander, not a single such pavement did he find. Cold they were, and hard they were, and dirty they were: dirtier by far, many of them, than the foulest country lane in Gloucestershire. All this he would never have minded had he come across a solitary chip of the precious metal. But not one did he find, nor a lost halfpenny either.

By midnight, his feet and legs were made of aches. His eyes were full of tears: though, stout-spirited lad that he was, he never allowed one to fall. At last, quite exhausted, he lay down in the side-doorway of a city merchant's house and fell sound asleep.

He was awakened early next morning by the clacking tongue of the merchant's cook as she opened the kitchen door to sample the day's weather. 'Away, you lazy lout!'

she cried. 'Do not seek to attach yourself to the good
merchant Alderman Fitzwarren, for it's well-known
he has a heart as soft as a pat of July butter, and is easily
taken in by any villain with a fancy story. Be off
with you, now!'

At that moment, who should descend to unbar the
iron-studded door to his vaulted store but Alderman
Fitzwarren himself.

'Why, you poor hungry and homeless fellow!' he
declared, instantly seeing how it was with Dick.
'Come in and eat and rest, and then you shall replace
my last kitchen-lad. Only yesterday, he went to sea as
cabin-boy in one of my trading ships. It is fate that
has led you to my door, my friend, and no mistake.'

If looks were daggers, Dick would have been stabbed to death by the one the cook now gave him. But she could do no other than her master's bidding.

As a result, of course, however hard Dick tried to please her with his work, the scowling cook was never satisfied. Many an undeserved blow she aimed at his head with a ladle or at his back with a broom-handle, declaring that one task was not properly finished, or that another was not performed at all. Dick, nevertheless, did his best to be undaunted by her hard words and her heavier hand. Only one thing cast down his spirits a little.

The attic-room where he lay at night was full of
holes made by rats and mice that came boldly out
and scampered and squeaked through the hours of
darkness. He could not sleep, and rose fit for nothing
every morning. However he might try and block the
holes, the creatures broke through ever and again.

'I know what I will do,' he said to himself suddenly,
as he wound the spit one dinner-time,
pinching his body to keep himself
awake, and fearful that the cook might
notice his weariness and have him put

out on the streets for failing to do his work properly. 'I will buy myself a cat. I will be kind to her, and she shall drive away the mice and rats that rob me of my slumber.'

So, the next day, and with the first penny of his wages, he bought himself a bonny little she-cat with a coat as shining and as black as the moonlit night-sky itself. Her pointed teeth and her powerful claws were like little swords and scimitars. Her tail was as thick as a church bell-rope, and her purr could be heard in the next room. Oh, but Dick was bothered with

neither rats nor mice after purchasing this pennyworth,
I can tell you!

Everyone grew to love Dick's cat for her beauty and
usefulness: except, of course, the cook, who always sent
the animal flying from the kitchen with a well-aimed ladle
or spoon. But Alderman Fitzwarren's pretty daughter
Alice, who from the goodness of her heart now took
Dick's part whenever the cook complained about him or
his work, saw to it that puss was kept out of trouble,
and that many an extra lap of milk and tasty morsel came
her way while Dick was busy in the kitchen.

Now there came a day when Alderman Fitzwarren's
ship the *Martlet* was to set sail from London Pool
to the coast of Morocco. As was the custom the good
Alderman invited his servants to send something
by her, in goods or gear, that they might enjoy a
share in the profits of the venture.

All prepared to do so save Dick, who had
neither gear nor goods of his own. Sorrowful

he was indeed that he could not so show his confidence in the affairs of a master who had done him nothing but kindness. But there was little that Dick could do about it: little, that is, until he recalled how the Alderman had often remarked on the rats and mice on ship-board, who plagued the crews, robbed them of their food, and damaged the cargoes so that sometimes a voyage seemed hardly worth the making. Ships' cats had been taken on, and a-plenty: but a ship's cat of real quality was rare indeed.

Then Dick thought of his own dear cat: a master-hunter, and a quite tireless one and no mistake. So, feeling he could do no other, and after explaining the matter to her as best as he was able, Dick offered her for the *Martlet*. At first, knowing how much the two friends loved each other, the Alderman was minded not to accept. But, wise man that he was, he realized that for Dick's sake he must do so: knowing that in his heart the lad was anxious to show him thanks.

With never a thought of reward, and with a bright tear resting on his cheek, Dick bade farewell to his friend: who, it must be said, scampered cheerfully enough up the gangway, having heard that there were as many rats and mice aboard ship as ever there were on land.

And with the very next penny he earned, Dick brought himself another cat – of a silky redness this time – that he might have a friend to care for, as well as continue to sleep well of nights. At this, the cook grew even more spiteful, beating him at every chance, and wounding his feelings with cries of, 'Hey boy, but are you training that cat to be a sailor too?'

Dick grew so unhappy that he resolved to endure such ill-treatment no longer. Rising well before sun-up, he packed his bundle. Then, taking Red Fur in his arms, for he feared what the cook might do to her when she found that he had gone, Dick crept out of the house, and the friends walked together as far as the village of Highgate.

As he dozed for a moment, resting against a stone at the foot of Highgate Hill, he heard, far but clear, the six bells of Bow church. To his astonishment, they seemed to say,

'Turn again, Whittington,
Thrice Lord Mayor of London.'

'Why,' said Dick to puss, whose ears had risen like twin steeples at the sound, 'now did you hear that, Red Fur? Thrice Lord Mayor, eh? I'm hanged if I'll be cheated of my fate and fortune by a crotchety cook. If I'm to be Lord Mayor, Lord Mayor I'll be. I can put up with a little sourness now for the sake of sweetness to come.'

So they marched resolutely back to Alderman Fitzwarren's before even the cook's head had risen from her pillow.

Meanwhile, the *Martlet* was nearing the coast of
Morocco, and before long anchored in the port of Rabat.
Immediately, the Captain received an invitation from the
Sultan of that country to attend, with all his ship's
company, a banquet in their honour
at the royal palace.

Putting on their best garments and wearing their ceremonial swords, the officers paraded the crew and all marched in procession, with a drummer at their head, to the palace. Here they were greeted with great politeness by the Sultan and his queen, the Sultana.

Having asked the guests to be seated, the Sultan struck his hands together, and a file of servants entered with an array of foods upon large silver and golden dishes, which they placed before the company. Then, as a signal that the meal was about to begin, a glittering gong at the Sultan's side was beaten by a slave.

But before a single morsel could be raised to the lips,
there was a great scurrying and scrambling of small feet.
To the amazement of the visitors. a horde of rats and
mice then rushed into the banqueting hall and gobbled
up every scrap of food. Finally, with a tremendous

squeaking, the creatures disappeared out of the
doors and windows through which they had
entered so swiftly.

'My friends,' the Sultan
announced sadly, 'it was
once the custom of my
country to entertain all
travellers as though they
were of our own blood.
Great is my sorrow, then,

that so overrun are we with mice and
rats that such a welcome now seems
impossible. Would that you were
able, by means of some strange wonder
you bring from your own land, to rid
my land of such a plague.'

At this, the Captain, the ablest and
most business-like of fellows, at once
called for the ship's boy, that very lad
whom Dick had replaced in Alderman
Fitzwarren's kitchen.

'Go,' commanded the Captain, 'and
bring Dick Whittington's cat, as has
been of such capital service on our
outward voyage. And see that she has
no supper before she leaves the vessel.'

The ship's boy, having been carried to and from the harbour on one of the Sultan's speediest Arab horses, was back in the banqueting hall in no time, and now with Dick's cat for company.

The Captain raised the lid of the basket in which she lay comfortably upon a little blanket one of the sailors had knitted for her. Up came puss's head: black ears cocked, whiskers stiff, eyes afire with interest and expectancy. She stepped delicately out onto a large, gold-coloured cushion. At the sight of the Sultan and his Queen, the Sultana, she gave a loud cry of interest.

'Bid your slave strike the gong as though a meal were about to begin, your majesty,' said the Captain, 'and you shall see what you shall see.'

The gong was struck, and at once a swarm of rats and mice darted into the room, at the centre of which the cat sat proudly, eyes burning.

Then, fast as a flash of light, she leapt among them and laid no less than three hundred low before the creatures realized what was happening. With teeth clashing, claws dashing, tail erect, she weaved this way and that among them, quicker than the human eye could follow. Those few lucky enough to escape her busy paws and jaws hurled themselves from the room, and out of the palace, before you could say 'Dick Whittington'.

As the last mouse skidded
frantically down the marble steps
and vanished into the night, the
cat turned in the entrance to the
hall and seized the lifeless figure of
the largest rat. Carrying it proudly
the length of the room, she laid the
body before the royal couple, who
clasped hands and danced together
for sheer joy.

'Come, your highness,' said the
Captain to the Sultana. 'Take puss
on your lap. Stroke her with
kindness to show your love for her.
She will then serve you faithfully

all her life, as well as the fine litter of kittens she will shortly present you with, I can promise.'

Without a moment's delay, the Sultan offered to buy not only the cat, but also the whole of the ship's cargo. Such was his delight that he insisted on paying five hundred times the price Dick had set upon his cat, as well as ten times that asked for every other item. In addition, he sent Dick an ivory casket filled with jewels, a ring for him to wear, and – on learning that the young man was still a bachelor – another to give his bride upon her wedding day.

Thirty days later, as Dick was toiling in Alderman Fitzwarren's kitchen, the old cook chiding him mercilessly the whiles, the thud of a cannon and a distant cheer warned him that a ship had at that moment dropped anchor in the river.

Great was the excitement in the household when it was learned that the vessel was none other than the *Martlet*. Even Dick dared to pause a moment in cleaning the roasting-spit, wondering if his cat had been of good service in his master's venture.

He had no need to wonder long, for within the hour, Alderman Fitzwarren had summoned Master Richard Whittington urgently into his presence.

'Master Richard Whittington?' asked Dick. 'I am no Master, sir, but only your poor scullion.'

'Scullion no longer,' said the Alderman, 'but Master Richard indeed, and a fine gentleman of substance and quality.'

And so it was that the amazed Dick was told of all that had happened: the momentary sadness

he felt that his friend had not returned being more than eased by the great joy of knowing that she was safe and healthy and happy, most highly regarded by the Sultan and Sultana and the whole kingdom of Morocco, and of the utmost service to the people of that country.

That evening, he dined with Alderman and Mistress Fitzwarren and their daughter Alice, and was afterwards shown not to his attic but to the chief guest-chamber.

Here, after quietly calling his
penny cat down from aloft, he
slept the night – and every
night thereafter until he set up a
splendid merchant's house for
himself. And there he lay in his
own four-poster, still with puss
curled up at the foot.

Soon, as you may guess,
Alice fell in love with the
handsome young merchant,
and Dick – who had long
wished to make Alice his bride,
but because of his poverty
had felt unable to declare it –
asked for her hand in marriage.

It was given gladly, and the wedding was one of the finest ever known in London, attended by many important and renowned citizens. Not least, it was watched by Dick's cat, who reminded her master always of that other four-footed friend who had served him so well, and upon whom his present fortune and happiness rested.

Puss watched proudly, too, as Dick –
or Sir Richard, as he had by then become
– drove in procession through the city
as its Lord Mayor: not once, not twice,
but three times, Once more the bells of
Bow church rang out, this time saying,

'Sir Richard Whittington
Lord Mayor has now become.'

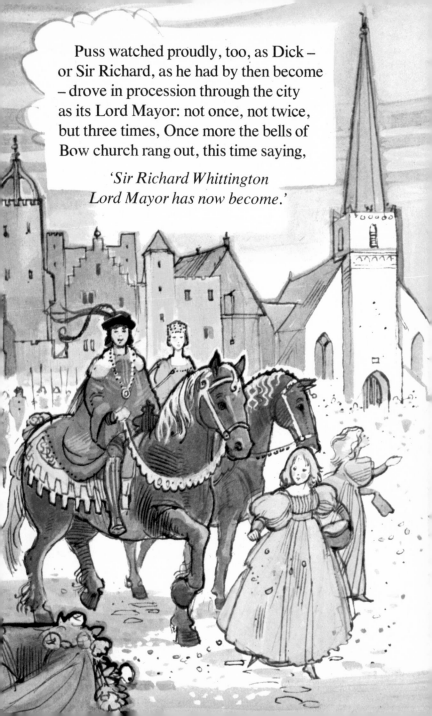

As Sir Richard and Lady Alice rode along on that first, famous occasion, it seemed to him that all the folk gathered along the streets – whether rich or poor, high or low – bowed and waved and smiled graciously as though each one was a great lady or gentleman. The houses gleamed like silver after the early-morning rain; and the pavements, in the fresh, morning sun, shone as if, at last, they were made of gold.

The End